For my wonderful Mam and Dad, with love – J G

To Daniel – T W

Copyright © 2010 by Good Books,
Intercourse, PA 17534
International Standard Book Number:
978-1-56148-697-7
Library of Congress Catalog Card Number:
2010004919

Text copyright © Magi Publications 2010
Illustrations copyright © Tim Warnes 2010

Original edition published in English by Little Tiger Press,
an imprint of Magi Publications, London, England, 2010.

LTP/1800/0047/0510 • Printed in China

Library of Congress Cataloging-in-Publication Data
Groom, Juliet.
Silent night / Juliet Groom ; [illustrated by] Tim Warnes.
p. cm.
Summary: Loosely based on the German Christmas song,
celebrates a wonder-filled night and the joys of nature.
ISBN 978-1-56148-697-7 (hardcover : alk. paper)
1. Children's songs--United States--Texts. [1. Nature--Songs.
2. Spiritual life--Songs. 3. Songs.] I. Warnes, Tim, ill. II. Title.
PZ8.3.G91Si 2010
782.28--dc22
2010004919

Silent Night

Juliet Groom　　Tim Warnes

Good Books
Intercourse, PA 17534
800/762-7171
www.GoodBooks.com

Silent night, holy night,
All is calm, all is bright.

All the animals gather together,

Silent, harmonious, happy forever.

Sleep in heavenly peace,
All **together** in peace.

Silent night, holy night,
Lift your hearts in joy tonight.

Take joy in our world, in the mountains so tall,
The flowers, so tiny — take joy in them all.

Celebrate all that we share,
Each precious moment we share.

Silent night, holy night,
Angels sing of love's pure light.

Love that brings a smile to each face,
That brightens each day with its
beauty and grace.

Cherish those dear to your heart,
Keep them safe, safe in your heart.

Silent night, holy night,
All the world holds its breath tonight.

High above, a **bright** star gleams,

A child is born, and heaven's gift brings . . .

. . . Hope for all in the world,

Hope for our beautiful world.